A Persian Passover

ETAN BASSERI

Illustrated by **RASHIN KHEIRIYEH**

Kalaniot Books
Moosic, Pennsylvania

To my family.

—E.B.

*Happy Passover to all who celebrate,
especially to Iranian-Jewish families.*

—R.K.

AUTHOR'S ACKNOWLEDGMENTS

This book would not be possible without the support and encouragement of my wife, Sonya. The story would never have come to life if my father, Jamshied Basseri, had not shared his experiences of growing up Jewish in Kermanshah, Iran.

Seattle Hebrew Academy teachers, including Lea Hanan, Katie Regala, and Nomi Winderbaum, provided critical early feedback from an educator's perspective. I am also incredibly grateful to my cousin Dr. Jaleh Pirnazar for her help in capturing key details of Jewish life in Iran during the mid-twentieth century. Any historical inaccuracies are either my own or a product of artistic license.

Finally, I want to thank Lili Rosenstreich of Kalaniot Books and Rashin Kheiriyeh for their incredible contributions in making this book a reality.

Text copyright © 2022 by Etan Basseri I Illustrations copyright © 2022 by Rashin Kheiriyeh

Published by Kalaniot Books, an imprint of Endless Mountains Publishing Company
72 Glenmaura National Boulevard, Suite 104B, Moosic, Pennsylvania 18507
www.KalaniotBooks.com

CIP Code: 0323/B2140/A6
Printed in China

Many years ago, in a small town in Iran, there lived a big brother and little sister, Ezra and Roza.

"Roza, count how long it takes for me to run around the house," shouted Ezra to his sister in the front yard.

"Ready, set, go!" she called, and he was off. "Good morning, Mrs. Pirnazar," Roza called across the courtyard to their neighbor who was busy hanging her tablecloths out to dry.

Mrs. Pirnazar answered with a quiet "Good morning, Roza *joon*."

Suddenly, Ezra turned the corner of the house and ran smack into Mrs. Pirnazar. "Oof! Sorry, Mrs. Pirnazar! I was just trying to see how fast I could make a lap around the house."

"That's okay, Ezra *joon*. Remember, it's good to be fast, but it's also important to be careful," she said with a smile.

"Forty-five seconds, Ezzy," called Roza as she ran over. "A new record! But you still need to work on your form, you know."

One bright spring day, while passing the synagogue on their way home from school, Roza was excited to see something she had never noticed before. "Ezzy! What are they building in the courtyard?"

Ezra explained, "That's the matzah oven. Every year for Passover, each family brings their own flour to the synagogue to be mixed, rolled, and baked into soft, delicious matzah. Now that you're old enough, you'll come with me when we return to make our very own."

The next day, the whole family was busy preparing for Passover. They swept the house, shook out the carpets, and gathered flowers from their garden.

Their kitchen was buzzing with activity: chopping, stirring, and simmering. As Roza passed by, she saw piles of dates, golden raisins, pistachios, almonds, and other ingredients that Mama would mix together later that day for *hallaq*, the Persian charoset used during the Passover seder.

After lunch, Ezra spotted the special sack of Passover flour his parents had bought. As he picked it up and walked out, he held his head high, feeling proud to have such an important job. After all, matzah is the only type of bread that can be eaten during the week of Passover.

He found Roza arranging flowers near the *sofreh*, where they would have their seder.

"Time for us to go make our matzah. Let's race there and see how long it takes!" said Ezra as they started down the street.

"Okay," replied Roza. "Ready, set, go!" Around corners, up the alleys, and across to the synagogue they ran.

Arriving at the synagogue courtyard, Roza exclaimed, "Eight minutes, Ezzy. Pretty fast! Hey, look at all of these people!" The courtyard was bustling. People were lined up with their flour, and a small group was gathered near the large brick oven, mixing, kneading, and baking.

When it was their turn, Ezra and Roza handed over their sack of flour to the team of bakers.

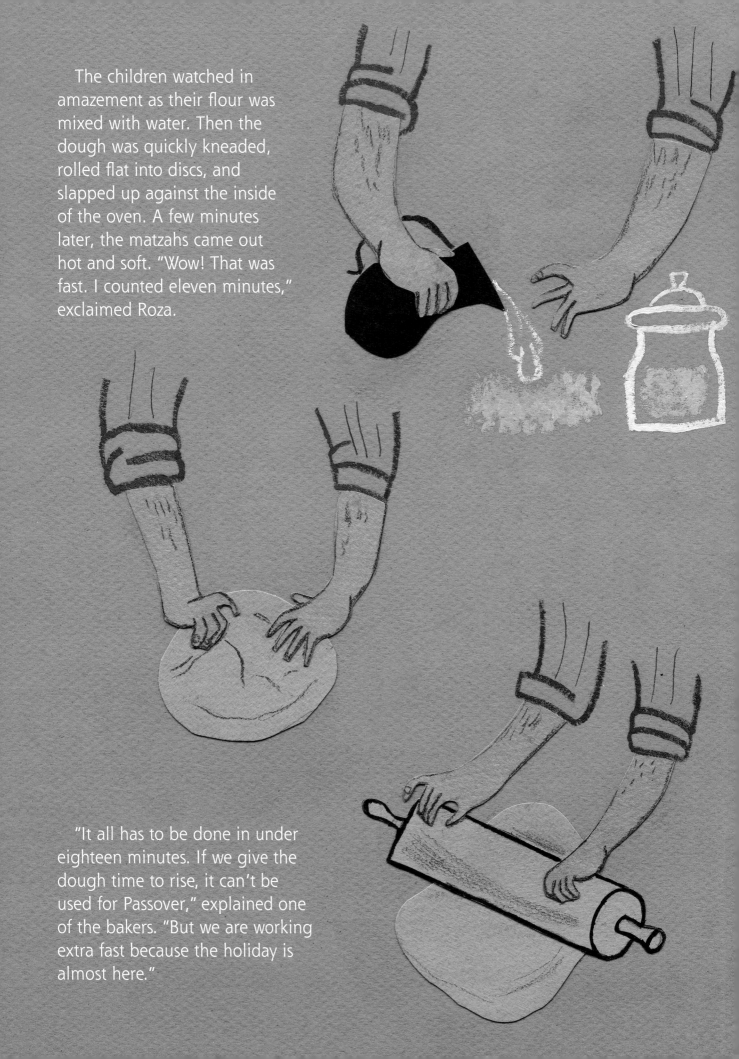

The children watched in
amazement as their flour was
mixed with water. Then the
dough was quickly kneaded,
rolled flat into discs, and
slapped up against the inside
of the oven. A few minutes
later, the matzahs came out
hot and soft. "Wow! That was
fast. I counted eleven minutes,"
exclaimed Roza.

"It all has to be done in under
eighteen minutes. If we give the
dough time to rise, it can't be
used for Passover," explained one
of the bakers. "But we are working
extra fast because the holiday is
almost here."

"Thank you. *Moadim shalom!* Have a nice holiday!"
replied Ezra and Roza, as they quickly wrapped their
matzahs with cloth to keep them warm. Ezra slung the
package over his shoulder and they set off for home.
"Roza, count how long it takes for me to race to the next
corner!" Ezra was off like a shot.

But he didn't see the rut in the road up ahead. "Oof!"
yelped Ezra as he tripped and fell. *Splat!* went the bag of
matzah as it dropped into a puddle.

"The matzah!" they exclaimed together.

"That was all the matzah we had for the week. Now it's gone. What will we tell Mama and Baba?" asked Roza.

"I don't know," Ezra cried.

"Wait," said Roza. "Let's try the market. Maybe one of Mama's or Baba's friends will help." Ezra took a deep breath, nodded, and off they marched.

The market was especially crowded today. Rows
of tables formed a sea of green piled high with herbs
and vegetables.

The smell of parsley, mint, tarragon, and dill wafted through the busy stalls as people hurried to make their final purchases before the market closed down for Passover.

"Excuse me, Mrs. Davidian, do you have any extra matzah?"
Roza asked.

"No, sorry. Not this close to Passover. Here, take some
scallions for when you sing 'Dayenu' during the seder. But
don't hit your brother too hard with them, Roza *joon!*"

"Oh, thank you, Mrs. Davidian. I'll be gentle, I promise,"
laughed Roza.

"Excuse me, Mrs. Roshan, do you have any extra matzah?" Roza asked.

"No, sorry. Why didn't you come yesterday? Here, take some candied almonds, Roza *joon*," was the answer.

"Thank you, Mrs. Roshan. This will make our Passover extra sweet," said Roza.

While the children now had scallions and candied almonds, no one at the market had any matzah to spare.

"Roza, let's go home," whispered Ezra as he hung his head. There was nothing left to do but tell his parents what had happened. He felt terrible.

They stopped outside the gates to their courtyard. Ezra was very nervous. As he thought about what to tell his parents, Mrs. Pirnazar walked by.

She smiled and said, "Children! Look at you helping out with errands before Passover. How are you? How are your parents?"
"Thank you, *khanoum.* Everything is fine," answered Ezra.

"It's not fine, Ezzy!" exclaimed Roza. Turning to Mrs. Pirnazar, she announced, "It is not fine at all!" And Ezra hung his head as Roza explained everything that had happened. "Now we have no matzah," she cried.

"Why, you are in luck." Mrs. Pirnazar laughed. "I happen to have plenty of matzah to share."

Ezra let out a gigantic sigh of relief. "Thank you so much, Mrs. Pirnazar. You saved our Passover! Are you sure you can spare this matzah?"

"It's okay, Ezra *joon*. I am celebrating alone this year," she said.

"But Mrs. Pirnazar, you MUST spend the seder with us!" pleaded Roza.

"Roza *joon*, you are sweet, but I couldn't impose myself on the eve of Passover."

"Mrs. Pirnazar, please come. We learned that anyone who is in need of a place for the seder is welcome. Let's celebrate together!"

Later that evening, Ezra and Roza, together with their parents and friends, sat around a large *sofreh* decorated with a seder plate, charoset, scallions, dyed eggs, and green sprouts. Mama turned to Mrs. Pirnazar. "Ezra told us about his accident. Thank you so much for helping us, *khanoum*. I'm so happy we can celebrate Passover together. Right, Ezra?"

"Yes, and I promise not to rush through the seder this year, Mama. It's good to be fast," Ezra said, with a look at Mrs. Pirnazar, "but it's also important to be careful."

Raising his glass of wine for the first cup, his father addressed the entire room of guests. "I want to welcome everyone to our seder. Made possible by our dear neighbor Mrs. Pirnazar. *Moadim shalom.*" Mrs. Pirnazar gave the children a smile and the seder began.

Passover

Passover is a holiday of stories and symbols that we celebrate every spring. During the Passover seder, we tell the story of how the Jews were slaves in Egypt, forced to build Pharaoh's cities, and how God freed them and gave them the Torah. Matzah is a symbol of freedom. When the Jews were escaping from Egypt, they had to leave in a hurry and could not wait for their dough to rise. They had to bake it in a flat bread and get out.

You can find many symbols of Passover on the seder plate.

Glossary

Dayenu (Hebrew): A song about the Exodus sung during the seder. Persian Jews have the tradition to hit each other with scallions during the song. This might refer back to the whips the Egyptian taskmasters used against the Jews when they were slaves, or when the newly-freed Jews complained to Moses about missing the onions and other bountiful foods of Egypt.

Hallaq (Persian) / **Charoset** (Hebrew): A sweet, dark paste made from dried fruits, nuts, and spices, eaten during the Passover seder.

Joon (Persian): Dear

Khanoum (Persian): Ma'am

Mama/Baba (Persian): Mom and Dad

Matzah (Hebrew): Unleavened bread eaten during Passover. Matzah must be made within 18 minutes so the dough cannot rise. In Iran, matzah is often baked in a clay-and-brick wood-burning oven. The matzahs are round, soft, and delicious.

Moadim shalom (Hebrew): A Persian-Jewish holiday greeting.

Seder (Hebrew): Order. A Jewish ritual service and dinner celebrated on Passover.

Sofreh (Persian): The arrangement of holiday symbols, traditionally on ornate fabric.

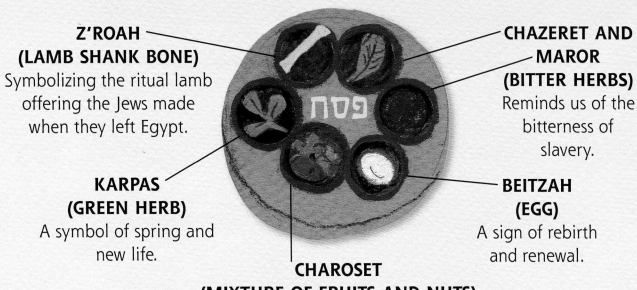

Z'ROAH (LAMB SHANK BONE)
Symbolizing the ritual lamb offering the Jews made when they left Egypt.

CHAZERET AND MAROR (BITTER HERBS)
Reminds us of the bitterness of slavery.

KARPAS (GREEN HERB)
A symbol of spring and new life.

BEITZAH (EGG)
A sign of rebirth and renewal.

CHAROSET (MIXTURE OF FRUITS AND NUTS)
Symbolizing the mortar that the Jews used to make bricks when they were slaves.

Jews in Persia

Jews have been living in the Middle Eastern region, known today as Iran, since the sixth century BCE. Back then, it was called the Persian Empire. Today, the culture and main language of this region is still called "Persian." In the 1950s, when this story takes place, Ezra and his family would have lived amongst the majority Muslim population. They would have spoken the Persian language, sometimes known as Farsi, as well as Judeo-Persian (a mix of Hebrew and Farsi) in their Jewish community. Today, many of those communities have immigrated to Israel and the United States, but some remain in Iran.

Just like there are many Passover customs particular to your own family, Persian Jews have special customs too. Some of these are a result of the influence of local culture, including the celebration of Nowruz, the Persian New Year, which is a spring festival, just like Passover. Colorful eggs are often used to decorate tables during this festival and therefore may find their way onto Passover tables as well, especially since we find eggs used in various ways already on Passover. The tradition of welcoming guests to our homes and dinner tables, which we find originally in the Torah, and trace back to Abraham and Sarah, is also a part of the Passover seder ("Anyone who is hungry, come and eat"), as well as part of Persian culture. When Roza learns that Mrs. Pirnazar is celebrating Passover alone, she invites her to join her family. In true Persian tradition, Roza does not take "no" for an answer. Is there someone you know who might need an invitation to your next seder?

Hallaq Recipe
PERSIAN-STYLE CHAROSET

Ingredients:

1 cup almonds
1 cup shelled pistachios
1 cup walnuts
1 cup hazelnuts
1 cup dried figs
1 cup dates
1 cup golden raisins
1.5 tsp. cinnamon
1.5 tsp. cardamom
1 apple
1 pear
Juice of 1 orange
Water as needed

Directions:

1. Combine nuts and spices in a food processor and blend until fine. Remove and set aside.

2. Peel and slice the apple and pear, then combine with the dried fruits and orange juice and blend in the food processor until smooth. Add a little water as needed.

3. Add the nuts gradually, blending and adding a little water at a time, as needed.

4. Refrigerate until ready to enjoy.

Adjust ingredients and measurements according to your taste.

Be sure to follow this recipe with the help of an adult.